Y0-BRG-786

I Hate Rules!

For Trina—N.K.
For Babette—J&W

If you purchased this book without a cover, you should be aware
that this book is stolen property. It was reported as "unsold
and destroyed" to the publisher, and neither the author nor the publisher
has received any payment for this "stripped book."

Text copyright © 2003 by Nancy Krulik. Illustrations copyright © 2003
by John and Wendy. All rights reserved. Published by Grosset & Dunlap,
a division of Penguin Young Readers Group, 345 Hudson Street,
New York, NY, 10014. GROSSET & DUNLAP is a trademark of
Penguin Random House LLC.
Manufactured in China

Library of Congress Cataloging-in-Publication Data

Krulik, Nancy E.
        I hate rules! / by Nancy Krulik ; illustrated by John & Wendy.
                p. cm. — (Katie Kazoo, switcheroo ; 5)
        Summary: Third-grader Katie Carew gets into trouble for
breaking school rules, but when she magically turns into the
school's principal and eliminates all rules, things get out of hand.
Includes directions for playing Four Square, Statue Tag, and Poison.
        [1. Schools—Fiction. 2. Behavior—Fiction. 3. Magic—Fiction.]
    I. John, ill. II. Wendy, ill. III. Title. IV. Series: Krulik,
Nancy E.
    Katie Kazoo, switcheroo ; 5.
    PZ7.K944Ih 2003
    [Fic]—dc21

2002015623

10 9 8 7 6 5 4 3 2 1

Proprietary ISBN 978-1-101-95131-6
Part of Boxed Set, ISBN 978-1-101-95128-6

I Hate Rules!

by Nancy Krulik • illustrated by John & Wendy

Grosset & Dunlap

Chapter 1

"Ouch!"

Katie Carew groaned when George Brennan tagged her. George was a lot bigger than Katie. Sometimes he tagged too hard.

"Gotcha, Katie Kazoo!" George shouted, using the special nickname he'd given her. "Now you're part of the chain."

Katie frowned. She was always the first one tagged when they played Train Tag. Katie wasn't a very fast runner.

But she wasn't a bad sport, either. She linked her arm through George's without complaining. Together, they ran after Miriam Chan.

"You're tagged!" George cheered as he bashed into Miriam's side.

Miriam rubbed her arm where George had tagged her. "How come you guys never go after Jeremy or Kevin?"

"Because they're too fast," George explained. "Join the train."

Miriam slipped her arm through Katie's. "Now who should we try to tag?" she asked.

George looked around the playground. Jeremy Fox was there. So was Mandy Banks. They were both really fast. George couldn't catch them on his own—never mind when he was running with Miriam and Katie.

Then Suzanne Lock strolled onto the playground. She was wearing cowboy boots and a skirt. That wasn't a great outfit for running. She'd be an easy catch. "Let's get Suzanne!" George answered.

George took off in Suzanne's direction. He pulled Katie and Miriam behind him.

"Gotcha!" Miriam and George cried out as

they reached Suzanne.

"Join the train," Katie added.

"No, thank you," Suzanne answered.

"What do you mean, 'No thank you'?" George demanded to know. "We tagged you, so you have to join the train."

"No I don't," Suzanne told him. "Train Tag is for kids."

"We *are* kids," George reminded her.

"Well, I've got more grown-up things to do." Suzanne reached into her pocket and pulled out a cell phone. "I have to make a call."

"Hey! Whose is that?" Miriam asked.

"Mine," Suzanne answered.

Katie had seen that phone before. It really belonged to Suzanne's dad. But Katie didn't say anything. She didn't want to embarrass her best friend.

"How come you brought your cell phone to school?" Miriam asked.

"You never know when you might need to

call someone," Suzanne told her.

"Hey, Katie Kazoo. You know what you get when you mix a telephone with a pair of scissors?" George asked.

"What?" Katie asked.

"Snippy answers!"

Katie giggled. She loved when George told jokes.

Suzanne didn't. Instead of laughing, she pulled a headset from her backpack. "I can talk on the phone and still use my hands," Suzanne explained. She plugged the headset into the phone.

"My mom has one of those in her office," Miriam told her. "You look really grown up, Suzanne."

Suzanne smiled.

Just then, Katie's other best friend, Jeremy Fox, came running over. "Hey! Mrs. Derkman is going to make us line up any minute. We don't have much time left to play. Come on!"

"You guys go ahead," Suzanne said. "I'll

just stay here with my phone."

But before the kids could go back to their game, Mrs. Derkman blew her whistle. "Class 3A," the teacher called out, "let's line up."

"Boy, that math homework was really hard," Katie whispered to Jeremy as they got in line.

"It took a long time," Jeremy agreed.

George looked at them both strangely.

"Math homework? We had math homework?"

"You didn't do it?" Katie asked.

George turned red in the face. "I . . . uh . . . I guess I forgot."

"Oh man," Jeremy moaned. "This stinks."

"Why?" Katie asked him. "*George* forgot his homework. Not you."

"I know," Jeremy agreed. "But George, you were supposed to be in the four-square championship at recess. You're the best four-square player in our whole class."

George smiled. "I'm the king. I'm going to destroy the kids in 3B."

Jeremy shook his head. "No you're not. You're not even going to be there. You know the rule. If you forget your homework, you have to do it at recess."

George didn't look so happy anymore. "Mrs. Derkman has too many rules," he moaned as he got into line.

Chapter 2

Katie walked into the classroom and hung her jacket on the third hook from the left.

Then she placed her homework in the bin on Mrs. Derkman's desk.

Finally, she sat down at her desk and began to copy the spelling words on the board.

Katie did the same thing every morning. Mrs. Derkman had very strict rules about how you behaved in her classroom.

George sniffed at the air as he put away his coat. "*Ooh*. Do you have tuna fish again, Manny? Or did you just forget to shower?"

A few kids chuckled. Mrs. Derkman did

not. "If you have a question, George, please raise your hand," she said.

George sat down quietly and pulled out his notebook.

Just then a small piece of paper landed on Katie's desk. It was a note from Suzanne. Katie read the note and scribbled an answer.

"Kevin, pass this to Suzanne?" Katie whispered as she folded the paper. Kevin sat between Katie and Suzanne.

"No way," he whispered back. "I'm not getting in trouble."

Katie frowned, but she understood. Mrs. Derkman didn't like kids passing notes in class. It wasn't Kevin's note. Why should he risk it?

Katie waited until Mrs. Derkman was looking the other way. Then she tossed the note to Suzanne.

Katie almost hoped Suzanne *wouldn't* write back. If Mrs. Derkman caught the girls writing notes, she was sure to do something

mean. Something absolutely horrible.
Something . . .

"Suzanne, give me that note," Mrs.
Derkman ordered.

Oh no! Mrs. Derkman had seen them.

Suzanne looked at Katie and bit her lip.
She didn't move. It looked like she was frozen.

"Suzanne, you heard me." Mrs. Derkman

held out her hand.

Suzanne stood up. She walked slowly toward the front of the room. All the kids were staring. All except Katie. She couldn't even look at her.

"Thank you," Mrs. Derkman said when Suzanne handed her the note. "Please go back to your seat."

Katie breathed a sigh of relief. That wasn't so bad.

But Mrs. Derkman wasn't finished. She opened the note and began to read it . . . *out loud!*

"My mother bought me these horrible pink flowery underpants. They're for babies." Mrs. Derkman read Suzanne's words.

Suzanne buried her

head in her arms.

"Do you have to wear them?" Mrs.
Derkman continued, reading Katie's part of
the note.

"I'm wearing them right now." Mrs.
Derkman said, as she read what Suzanne had
just written.

The teacher looked at Suzanne and Katie.
"I don't think that was so important that it
couldn't wait until lunch. Do you girls?"

At first no one in the class said anything.

Then, a few of the boys started to giggle. Soon, everyone was laughing really hard.

"Pink flower underpants," Manny Gonzalez howled. "Real stylin', Suzanne!"

"I see England, I see France, I see Suzanne's flower underpants," George began to chant.

Suzanne looked like she was about to cry. "I wish I could hide under a big rock," she moaned quietly.

Katie looked up at the ceiling. What if a giant rock really did come falling down? What if it landed right on Suzanne's head?

But no rock fell from the sky. In fact, nothing happened at all. Katie breathed a sigh of relief. Suzanne had been lucky. Her wish hadn't come true.

Katie knew all about wishes that came true. She knew you had to be careful what you wished for. Not all wishes turned out great.

It had all started one really bad day. Katie

had ruined her favorite jeans and burped in front of the whole class. Katie had wished that she could be anyone but herself.

There must have been a shooting star flying overhead or something when Katie made her wish because the very next day, a magic wind blew. It was like a tornado that stormed just around Katie. The wind turned Katie into Speedy, the class hamster! That had been awful. Katie had been completely naked—except for Speedy's fur, of course.

Luckily, Katie had changed back into herself before anyone realized who was really chomping on Speedy's chew sticks. *Un*luckily, the magic wind returned. That time it turned Katie into Lucille, the school's lunch lady. She'd had to serve the kids gloppy egg salad and old milk. *Blech!*

Even that wasn't as bad as the time the magic wind turned Katie into Suzanne's baby sister, Heather. Eating cafeteria food tasted good compared to sucking smelly baby formula from a bottle.

The weirdest thing the magic wind ever did was turn Katie into Jeremy Fox. That had been a real mess. Katie hadn't known whether to go to the boys' room or the girls' room. Even worse, she'd almost lost Jeremy as a friend.

The magic wind hadn't been back for a while. But Katie had a feeling it wasn't through with her yet. She couldn't be sure when the wind would come, or who it would turn her into next.

That's why Katie didn't make wishes anymore. You never knew what could happen if they came true.

Chapter 3

Miriam Chan sat down at the cafeteria table beside her best friend, Mandy Banks. "Come on, let's do 'I Wanna Send a Letter,'" she said before she even unpacked her lunch.

Mandy swallowed a bite of her egg salad sandwich and nodded. Then the two girls stood up and began playing a new clapping game.

"Mail a letter to a boy from camp, camp, camp.
Seal the envelope with a stamp, stamp, stamp.
He's the one I always miss, miss, miss,
So I seal it with a kiss, kiss, kiss.
Hope he gets it in a snap, snap, snap,
And sends a note to make me clap, clap, clap."

Everyone watched as Miriam and Mandy

played their new game. The girls stamped
their feet when they said 'stamp,' missed when
they said 'miss,' blew kisses, snapped their fingers, and clapped their hands.

"Hey, can you teach me that?" Katie asked
when the girls finished.

"Sure. I'll show you after lunch," Mandy
agreed.

"Me too?" Zoe Canter asked.

"Of course," Miriam said. "We can do it while we watch the four-square championship."

"I think my mother used to play a game like that," Suzanne told the others. She reached into her pocket and pulled out her cell phone. " I'll call her and find out."

But before Suzanne could dial her mother, George grabbed the phone from her hands. He raced to the other side of the table and began to push numbers on the phone.

"Who are you calling?" Suzanne cried.

"It doesn't matter," George replied. "I'm just calling anyone."

"It better not be long distance," Suzanne told him.

George ignored her. "Hello," he said to the person who answered the phone. "Is your refrigerator running?" When the person on the other end said yes, George started giggling. "Then you'd better catch it!" he exclaimed.

George tossed the phone to Katie.

"You've got to hear this, Katie Kazoo!" he shouted.

Katie reached up and caught the phone. She could hear the woman screaming on the other end. "You shouldn't make phony phone calls," Katie told George.

"Especially on *my* phone," Suzanne added.

Just then, Mr. Kane, the principal, walked over to their table. "What have you got there, Katie?" he demanded.

Katie gulped. He sounded really mad. "It's a phone," she said quietly.

"I can see that," Mr. Kane said. "It's against the rules for students to bring cell phones to school."

"This isn't . . ." Katie was about to say that the phone wasn't hers. Then she looked at Suzanne. She seemed like she was about to cry. Katie just couldn't tell Mr. Kane that the phone belonged to Suzanne. Suzanne had had a bad enough day—with her flower underpants and all.

Mr. Kane took the phone from Katie's hands. "You'll get this back at the end of the day."

"Yes sir," Katie said quietly. She turned to sit back in her seat.

But Mr. Kane wasn't finished. "You broke the rules, Katie," he continued. "You'll have to miss recess today. You can spend the time thinking about why we have rules in school."

Mr. Kane walked away. Katie could feel her face getting redder and redder. Everyone was staring at her.

And it wasn't even her fault.

The worst part was now she wouldn't get to learn Mandy and Miriam's clapping game. Everyone would know it but her.

"I hate rules!" Katie declared angrily.

Chapter 4

Katie sat at the empty cafeteria table and looked toward the window. The sun was shining brightly. She could hear the other kids playing outside. They sounded like they were having a lot of fun.

The weather was so nice that Mrs. Derkman had gone to sit on the steps just outside the cafeteria door. That way, she could be outside and still make sure George and Katie didn't get out of their punishment.

Katie took a big, angry bite from a carrot stick. This whole thing was so unfair!

"Hey, Katie Kazoo, how come you can't eat carrots with fingers?" George shouted. He was sitting at a table all the way on the other side of the room.

"Why?" Katie answered.

"Because carrots don't *have* fingers!" George laughed hard at his own joke.

Katie didn't laugh at all. She was too mad. This was all George's fault. "Which end of a carrot is the left end?" George tried another joke.

"I don't know."

George smiled. "The end you don't eat!"

Katie scowled.

"Come on! That one was funny," George said.

Katie shook her head. There was no way she was going to laugh at any of George's jokes today. "Aren't you supposed to be doing math?" she asked before he could tell her another one.

"Oh yeah," George replied. He looked around the table. "I guess I forgot my math book."

Katie couldn't believe it. "You'd better get that book. Mrs. Derkman will really be mad if you don't do the homework," Katie warned.

George couldn't argue with that. "I'll be right back!" Quickly he dashed out of the cafeteria and ran toward room 3A.

Now Katie was all alone. She looked up at the clock on the wall. There were still fifteen minutes of recess to go.

Just then, Katie felt a warm breeze nip at the back of her neck. *Uh-oh!* Mrs. Derkman must be coming back inside. She was going to be really mad that George had left.

Katie turned quickly toward the door. Mrs. Derkman wasn't there. In fact, the door was closed. But the wind was still blowing on the back of Katie's neck. And it wasn't blowing anywhere else in the room.

Katie gulped. She knew what that meant. This was no ordinary wind. This was the magic wind!

The magic wind began spinning faster and faster all around Katie. Her red hair whipped wildly around her head. She shut her eyes tightly, and tried not to cry. As the fierce tornado swirled, she held on to the table and struggled to keep her feet on the floor.

And then it stopped. Just like that. No warning. But Katie wasn't surprised. The magic wind *never* gave any warning. It didn't follow any rules.

Katie was glad that the tornado was over. But she was also very afraid. After all, whenever the wind stopped blowing, Katie turned into someone else.

Slowly, Katie opened her eyes and looked around. Right across from her was the huge mural she and her friends had painted on the cafeteria wall. It was a picture of unicorns riding skateboards over a rainbow.

Okay, so now she knew where she was. But she still didn't know *who* she was.

Katie looked at the tables and chairs in the cafeteria. They suddenly seemed small to her. She glanced down at her hands. They were really big . . . and kind of hairy! Yuck! the nails were all chewed down.

Who was she?

Before Katie could figure it out, George came racing back into the cafeteria. "Hey, Katie Kazoo . . . he began. Then he looked around, surprised. He didn't see his friend anywhere.

"Hi, Mr. Kane," he said. "Where did Katie go?"

Chapter 5

Mr. Kane? Was it possible? Had the magic wind actually turned Katie into the school principal?

Katie looked down. Instead of her T-shirt with the heart on it, she was wearing a white shirt and a navy blue striped tie. Her skirt was gone, too. A pair of gray wool slacks was in its place.

Katie reached up and touched her head. There was a big bald spot where her hair used to be. And when she opened her mouth to speak, a man's deep voice came out. "Katie? I . . . um . . . well . . . I don't know where she is," she told George.

"You mean she skipped out on her punishment?" George sounded impressed.

"I'd better go find her," Katie said quickly. She ran out of the cafeteria and into the hall.

The hallway was very noisy. The kids were coming back inside from recess.

"Hey, Mr. Kane," a fifth-grader named Sam greeted her.

"Hello," Katie said in her deep voice.

"Excuse me, Mr. Kane." Ms. Lobel, a kindergarten teacher, stopped Katie. "Do we still have that faculty meeting after school?"

Katie didn't know what to say. She didn't know anything about faculty meetings. "I . . . uh . . . I'll have to check," she said quickly.

Before she could take another step, Mr. Bloom, a second-grade teacher, came up to her. "Mr. Kane, were you able to look at my supply request form yet?"

"Supply request form?" Katie asked him. She'd never heard of one of those.

Mr. Bloom looked upset. "I really need

those extra notebooks," he said.

"I guess you should get them, then," Katie told him nervously.

"You have to sign the form," Mr. Bloom reminded her. "I'll come by for it later."

Katie knew she had to get out of the hall-way before she bumped into anyone else. Everyone thought she was Mr. Kane. They expected her to act like a real principal. But Katie had absolutely no idea what a real prin-cipal did.

Katie needed a place to hide until the magic wind came and turned her back into herself. But where could she go?

Just then, Mrs. Davidson, the school secre-tary, poked her head out of the office. "Mr. Kane," she said, "I left your messages on your desk."

That was it! Katie could hide out in Mr. Kane's office. After all, she *was* the principal.

"Um, thank you," Katie said, trying to sound very principal-like. "I'll get them now."

She dashed into Mr. Kane's office and shut the door.

Katie sat down behind Mr. Kane's big wooden desk and breathed a sigh of relief. At least no one could get to her in here.

She looked around the office. There were crowded bookshelves and stacks of paper everywhere. It looked kind of like Katie's dad's office, except Mr. Kane had wind-up toys on the windowsill, and there was a glass jar filled with chocolates on his desk.

Katie took one of the candies and popped it in her mouth. She leaned back in Mr. Kane's big leather chair and let the chocolate melt on her tongue. This wasn't so bad. She had plenty of snacks to eat, and toys to play with. As long as she stayed in Mr. Kane's office, she couldn't get into any trouble.

Well, that wasn't exactly true. Katie was actually going to be in *a lot* of trouble—as soon as Mrs. Derkman noticed that she wasn't in class. Katie didn't know what the punishment was for that, but she bet it was pretty bad. She *was* breaking a really big rule.

Now Katie was really worried. What if Mrs. Derkman called her mother? What if she called the police? How would Katie ever be able to explain what had happened to her?

Just then, Katie heard Mrs. Davidson's voice come over the loudspeaker. "All students should be in class now."

That gave Katie a great idea. She knew how to make sure she wasn't breaking any rules. Quickly, she leaped up from the chair and ran to the outer office.

"I need to say something," Katie told Mrs. Davidson as she grabbed for the microphone.

"This is Mr. Kane," Katie announced. "From now on, there is one rule in Cherrydale Elementary School. And that rule is . . . *there are no rules!*"

Chapter 6

At first, the whole school was completely silent. It was as if no one could believe what they had just heard. Then, suddenly, the classroom doors burst open. Kids raced into the halls.

"We're free!" a small girl with pigtails screamed out.

"Last one on the playground is a rotten egg!" yelled a tall, skinny second-grader.

"No rules, rules! No rules, rules! No rules, rules!" a group of fourth-graders chanted as they ran down the hall.

As Katie peeked out of the school office, a crowd of fifth-grade girls spotted her. "Wow.

It's Mr. Kane!" they squealed. "Thank you! Thank you!"

The students were treating Katie like some sort of rock star. As she strolled down the halls of the school, kids of all ages high-fived her. Some ran over to hug her. Katie smiled proudly. She was a hero.

Well, at least the *kids* thought she was a hero. The teachers had a different idea.

"Class 3A, come back here right now!" Mrs. Derkman shouted as her students streamed into the hallway. "It's not recess!"

But the kids didn't come back. Why should they? There was no rule that said they had to be in class.

"Mr. Kane!" Mrs. Derkman called out.

At first Katie jumped. Mrs. Derkman's angry voice scared her. Then Katie remembered. *She* was the principal. That made her Mrs. Derkman's boss.

Katie liked that idea a lot.

"Yes, Mrs. Derkman?" Katie answered. She

tried to sound very official.

"What's going on here?" Mrs. Derkman asked. "My class is going crazy."

"Relax," Katie told the teacher. "They're just having fun."

Before Mrs. Derkman could answer, a huge group of sixth-graders came running by at top speed. They were going so fast, they didn't even see Mrs. Derkman standing in their path. *Whoosh.* The teacher was swept away with the crowd.

"We'll talk about this later, Mr. Kane," Mrs. Derkman shouted as the sixth-grade mob pushed her down the hall.

Katie chuckled as she walked into the cafeteria. She peeked her head into the room. George was still the only kid there. But he wasn't struggling with math homework anymore. He was eating chocolate cake. Lots of chocolate cake.

Usually kids were only allowed one dessert with lunch. Right now, George had at least

ten pieces in front of him. And lunchtime had been over a long time ago.

"Looks like you're having fun," Katie said to George.

"*Mmmph. Phllmph.*" George mumbled through a mouthful of cake. Every time he opened his mouth, more wet, half-eaten chocolate crumbs poured out.

Watching George talk and chew was really gross. "Don't speak, George," Katie told him. "Just eat."

George gave her a big, chocolatey smile, then dove into his next slice of cake.

Suddenly, a whole group of kids came racing into the cafeteria. Jeremy was at the front of the crowd. He held a soccer ball in his hands.

"Where are you all going?" Katie asked them.

"To the yard, Mr. Kane," Jeremy explained with a huge smile. "We're going to play soccer all afternoon."

"Have fun!" Katie told him. She was glad she could make her best friend so happy.

Just then Katie heard laughing—and crying—coming from the computer lab across the hall. She raced to see what was happening.

Inside the lab, Suzanne, Mandy, Zoe, and Miriam were all staring at a picture on one of the computer screens. Suzanne, Mandy, and Miriam were smiling. Zoe was crying.

"What's wrong, Zoe?" Katie asked.

"Oh, don't worry about her, Mr. Kane,"

Suzanne said. "She always gets that way when she thinks about the Bayside Boys."

"We're looking at their official website," Mandy explained. "They just added a bunch of new pictures."

"Sammy looks so cute with curly hair," Zoe sobbed. "And J.T. is wearing the most adorable shorts!"

"Really? Let me see!" Katie said excitedly.

She edged Miriam over so she could get a better look at the screen.

The girls gave Katie a strange look.

"*You* like the Bayside Boys, Mr. Kane?" Suzanne asked.

Oops. Katie had almost forgotten that she was the principal. It must have seemed really weird to the girls that a grown man would be so interested in a pop group.

"No. I mean . . . well . . . um . . . gotta go!" Katie said quickly. She dashed out of the computer lab just as Kevin and Manny came running in.

"Mr. Kane, you're my favorite grown-up," Kevin said.

"Yeah. We're going to play Castle Craze now," Manny added. "It's so cool to be able to play computer games at school."

"Have a great time," she told the boys. "Remember, the best way to get to the fourth level is to capture the magic dragon."

"Wow!" Kevin exclaimed as Katie walked

away. "Mr. Kane knows how to play Castle Craze. How cool!"

"He's awesome," Manny agreed.

Katie smiled to herself. She didn't know when the magic wind was going to blow and turn her back into herself. But whenever that happened, Mr. Kane would be really happy. Katie had made him the most popular principal in the whole history of principals. The kids were so happy. Cherrydale Elementary School was the best school in the country. Maybe even in the whole *world*!

"*Owwww.*" Just then Katie heard George's voice. It sounded like he was in pain.

"Help me," he groaned. "Please."

Chapter 7

Katie found George in the hall just outside the nurse's office. He was curled up in a ball, moaning.

"What's wrong?" Katie asked him.

"My stomach hurts," George answered. "I think I ate too much."

"How many pieces of chocolate cake did you have?"

George made a face when Katie mentioned the cake. "I don't know. Maybe thirteen or fourteen slices."

"George!" Katie shouted out. "That's an awful lot of cake."

"Uh-oh," George murmured. He grabbed

his stomach. His face looked a bit green.

Katie jumped out of the way. "Nurse Hanes," she called out. "George needs help."

"So do the rest of these kids," Nurse Hanes shouted from inside her office.

Katie walked into the nurse's office. There was a huge line of kids. Some had cuts and bruises. Others were sitting with ice packs on their knees and heads. "What's going on?" Katie asked.

"It's this 'no rules' thing," the nurse explained. "These kids were running in the halls and playing with all sorts of gym equipment. It was just a matter of time before someone got hurt. How am I going to take care of all these kids?"

Katie was about to answer, when a first-grader ran up and pulled on her pants. "Mr. Kane, hurry. There's gonna be a fight."

"A fight? Where?" Katie asked nervously.

"On the soccer field," the boy answered. "Jeremy's real mad. So's Ricky."

That wasn't good. It took a lot to get Jeremy angry.

Quickly, Katie grabbed a trash can and placed it near George's head. "If you feel sick, use that. I gotta go."

Katie dashed out of the school. She could hear the boys screaming as she ran toward the soccer field. Coach G. was blowing his whistle over and over. The boys weren't listening.

"What's going on?" Katie asked the gym teacher.

"It's the 'no rules' rule," Coach G. told her. "It's ruined the whole game."

Jeremy came running over. "Mr. Kane, can't we just have rules for soccer?" he begged.

"No way," Ricky Dobbs argued. He looked up at Katie. "You said 'no rules.' That means no rules anywhere."

"But you're using your hands in soccer," Jeremy said. "You can't do that unless you're the goalie. And you're not the goalie."

"There's no rule saying I can't use my hands. Not anymore," Ricky argued.

"You see what I mean?" Coach G. asked Katie. He handed her his whistle. "Maybe you should be the referee for this game. I can't figure out who's winning in a game with no rules."

Before Katie could answer, Suzanne came running out to the field. "Mr. Kane, you'd better come to the computer lab. We were using all the computers at once. Now none of the computers are working—and the lights are out all over the school.

"Oh no!" Katie moaned. She followed Suzanne back into the dark school building. As she opened the door, a stream of green paint came flying toward her. It splattered all over Mr. Kane's white shirt. Katie looked down at the stain. The principal wasn't going to like this.

"What's going on in here?" Katie yelled.

"Paint fight," a sixth-grade girl named Justine told her. Justine ducked down to avoid being hit by a paint splatter. The red paint landed on Katie's bald head instead.

"How did this start?" Katie asked her.

"We took some supplies from the art room, and went to paint in the cafeteria," Justine explained. "Rachel's paint wound up on Dylan's jeans. So she painted his hair blue. After that, everyone got into it."

Katie sighed. This was not working out the way she'd thought it would. "Is the cafeteria a mess?" she asked.

"Not too bad," Justine answered. "There's a little paint on the walls. The mural's kind of messed up."

Oh, no. Not the mural Katie and her

friends had worked so hard on! Katie felt like she was about to cry. But she couldn't. Not here anyway. It wouldn't be good for the kids to see their principal cry.

Katie began running down the hall. She had to get to Mr. Kane's office right away. She could be alone there.

Whoosh! Katie slipped on a wet paint spot. She landed on her rear end and slid down the hall. A couple kids giggled.

Katie didn't feel like laughing at all.

Chapter 8

Katie raced into Mr. Kane's office and
slammed the door. She began to cry. It all was
too much for a third-grade girl to handle. If
only she were a real principal. Mr. Kane
would know what to do. Katie was sure of it.

Just then, a small breeze floated through
the office. The warm air tickled the back of
Katie's neck. Katie reached over to grab the
pile of papers on Mr. Kane's desk. She didn't
want them to blow away.

But the papers weren't moving. Nothing in
the office was.

Katie knew what that meant. The magic
wind was back!

The wind began to grow stronger. It whipped around Katie so fast that it made a slight whistling sound as it blew. Katie was scared, but she didn't cry. Instead, she called out, "Please, please, please let me turn back into me! I just want to be Katie Carew again!"

Then the wind stopped suddenly. Katie looked around. She wasn't in Mr. Kane's office anymore. She was back in the cafeteria, where the whole mess had started.

Of course the cafeteria didn't look like it had back during recess. Now there were paint stains on the walls and pieces of cake ground into the floors.

Katie looked down at her clothes. Instead of Mr. Kane's white shirt and gray slacks, she was wearing her heart T-shirt and her skirt. She felt the top of her head. She had her hair. Good.

Katie Carew was back.

Just then, Suzanne came running up to her. "Where've you been, Katie?" she asked.

"I've been looking all over for you."

Katie wasn't sure what to say. Suzanne wouldn't believe the truth even if she told her. Who would?

"Oh, I've been around," Katie said finally.

"This has been some crazy day," Suzanne said. "Mr. Kane sure surprised everyone with this no rules thing."

Katie nodded. She had a feeling that no one was more surprised by it than Mr. Kane himself.

"I'm just glad today's over," Katie told her. She began to walk toward the front door of the school. It was time to go home.

"By the way, thanks for not telling Mr. Kane that the phone was mine," Suzanne said, as the two girls walked outside.

"It's okay," Katie assured her.

"Maybe we should ask for my phone back," Suzanne said as the girls left the school. "He said you could have it at the end of the day."

Katie looked over at the principal. He was

sitting on the front steps of the building. He looked like a mess. The parents he was talking to seemed really angry.

"I'd wait until tomorrow, Suzanne," Katie suggested.

"I don't understand how you let this happen," Katie heard Kevin's mother say.

"I'm not sure, either, Mrs. Camilleri," Mr. Kane admitted.

"Didn't you tell the students there were no rules in school?" Mrs. Chan asked.

Mr. Kane looked confused. "I don't know. I mean, I must have. But I don't really remember doing it."

"I think you need a rest, Mr. Kane," Mrs. Dobbs said in an angry voice. "A long rest."

Katie gulped. Mrs. Dobbs was the president of the school's PTA. If she was mad, Mr. Kane could be in real trouble.

Chapter 9

The next morning, things on the play-ground seemed really weird. No one was playing. No one was laughing. No one was saying a word. Instead, the kids were standing in straight lines.

"What's going on?" Katie asked Manny as she took a place in line.

"Shhh," Manny whispered. "Do you want to get us in trouble?"

"Trouble?" Katie asked. "School hasn't even started yet."

"You. Come here!" A tall, skinny man with a small moustache called out.

"Who's that?" Katie asked Manny.

Before Manny could answer, the skinny man walked over to Katie. "Why are you talking?" he asked.

Katie didn't know what to say.

"We have a new rule here, Miss," the man said. "Students will line up quietly before school."

"Why?" Katie asked him.

"Because I said so," he replied. "And I'm your substitute principal, Mr. Ditherspoon. Everyone does what I want them to do."

Katie didn't say anything after that.

Mr. Ditherspoon looked at the students lined up before him. "There are going to be a lot of changes here," he told them. "For starters, there are new hair rules." Mr. Ditherspoon walked over to Caleb Connor, a sixth-grader who always wore big spikes in his hair. "You may not wear hair gel to school anymore. No one can. And girls with long hair must wear braids."

Katie didn't like the sound of that. Her hair was sometimes knotty and kind of curly. That made it really hard to braid.

"There will be no more T-shirts with words and pictures on them, either. Also, no more glitter—on your clothes or your faces. I want plain clothes and clean skin in my school."

Suzanne looked very upset. Everything she wore had glitter on it. With this new rule, she wouldn't have any school clothes at all.

"Okay, I want all of you to walk *silently* to class," Mr. Ditherspoon said as he opened the school doors. "Your teachers will fill you in on the rest of my new rules."

"You mean there are more?" George blurted out.

Mr. Ditherspoon glared at him. "I'll be watching you, Mr. Brennan," he growled.

Katie walked into her classroom, hung up her coat, put her homework on the pile, and sat at her desk. She pulled out a pencil and her notebook. But before she could begin her work, Mrs. Derkman pulled the pencil from her hand.

"This pencil point is too long," Mrs. Derkman said. She held up a ruler. "Mr. Ditherspoon doesn't want any pencil point to be more than one quarter inch long." She picked up Katie's notebook. "And from now on, every student must have plain black-and-white notebooks."

Katie looked down. She loved her notebook. On the cover, it had a picture of a puppy and a kitten in a basket. She didn't want a plain black-and-white notebook.

But that was the rule.

※※※※

At lunchtime, Katie slowly slid her tray along the line. When it was her turn, she smiled at Lucille the Lunch Lady. "I'll have the peas, the mashed potatoes, a glass of milk, and some rice pudding."

Lucille shook her head. "Sorry. You can't have dessert unless you eat the whole meal. And today we have hamburgers."

"But I don't eat meat," Katie told her.

"Then you don't eat pudding, either," Lucille told her. "That's Mr. Ditherspoon's rule."

Katie sighed. "Just the peas, the potatoes, and the milk, then." She took her tray and walked toward her class's table.

"Move over," she whispered to Jeremy. Katie wasn't sure if they were still allowed to talk at lunch. Nobody else seemed to be saying anything.

Jeremy slid his chair over and made room

for Katie. He took his fork and began to mush his peas together with his mashed potatoes.

Just then, Mr. Ditherspoon appeared at his side. "What are you doing with those peas?" he asked.

"Mixing them with my potatoes," Jeremy explained.

"You can't do that."

Jeremy pushed his glasses up on his nose nervously. "But I always eat them that way," he said quietly.

Mr. Ditherspoon glared at Jeremy. "There's only one way to eat at this school. And that's my way. If you want that dessert, you have to eat the hamburger, then the peas, then the mashed potatoes. There will be no mixing foods at my school!"

"Yes, sir," Jeremy mumbled quietly. He picked up his burger and took a bite.

"And make sure you chew each bite twenty-three times . . . exactly," Mr. Ditherspoon told him.

Jeremy chewed.

Katie looked around at her friends' sad faces. This was all her fault. If she hadn't gotten rid of all the rules at school, Mr. Kane would still be the principal. Things were really horrible now. And there didn't seem to be anything she could do about it.

Chapter 10

When Katie got home, she ran right up to her room and slammed the door. She was in a terrible mood. This had been the worst day ever. Katie's chocolate-and-white cocker spaniel, Pepper, scratched at her door. But Katie didn't open it. She didn't want to see anyone. Not even Pepper.

The phone rang downstairs. "Katie, it's for you," her mom called out.

Katie frowned. She really didn't feel like talking to any of her friends. "Who is it?" she asked.

"Suzanne," her mother answered. "She says it's important."

Katie ran downstairs and took the phone from her mother. "What?" she asked in a grumpy voice.

"Hello to you, too," Suzanne teased.

"I'm sorry," Katie apologized. "I'm just in a bad mood. Today was awful."

"Oh, yeah!" Suzanne agreed. "And it's going to get worse."

"What do you mean?"

"We might have Mr. Ditherspoon as our principal forever," Suzanne said.

"I thought he was just a substitute," Katie told her.

"He is," Suzanne agreed. "But my mom says the PTA is thinking about recommending him as our new principal."

"What about Mr. Kane?"

"There's going to be a big school board meeting on Friday. They might fire Mr. Kane," Suzanne told Katie.

"We have to stop them!" Katie exclaimed.

"Forget it, Katie. This is the *school board*.

They're not going to listen to kids," Suzanne told her.

"I'm not so sure about that. Remember, that's what you said when Mr. Kane fired Lucille," Katie reminded her. "But we got her job back for her."

It was true. Mr. Kane had fired the lunch lady after she'd gotten into a foodfight with some of the kids. Of course, it had actually been *Katie* who had gotten into the foodfight, but Mr. Kane didn't know that. He didn't know about the magic wind. The kids had saved Lucille's job by refusing to eat the cafeteria food until Mr. Kane hired her back.

"That's true," Suzanne said. "But I have no idea how we can get Mr. Kane back. Do you?"

Katie thought about it for a minute. Then she smiled. "I think I do. Will you help me?"

"Sure," Suzanne agreed. "I'll do anything to be allowed to wear glitter again!"

Chapter 11

As Katie walked into the school board meeting, her stomach was very jumpy. Some people might say she had butterflies in her tummy. But Katie thought they felt more like elephants. A whole herd of elephants . . . stampeding!

"Are you scared?" Jeremy whispered to Katie as they took their seats.

"Are you?" Katie asked.

Jeremy nodded. "I've never spoken in front of this many grown-ups before."

Katie looked over to where Suzanne was sitting with her parents. Even *she* looked nervous.

The meeting seemed to drag on forever. Lots and lots of grown-ups gave long speeches about how awful Mr. Kane's no-rules day was.

Mr. Kane didn't say anything. He just sat in the front of the room, looking very confused. Every now and then he wiped a bead of sweat from his forehead.

"Does anyone else have anything to say before we vote?" the head of the school board, Mr. Rosen, asked finally.

Katie raised her hand shyly.

"Yes?" Mr. Rosen pointed toward Katie.

Katie gulped. Everyone was staring at her. It was really scary. But Katie knew she had to say something. She had to save Mr. Kane.

Katie walked up to the front of the room. "My name is Katie Carew," she said. "I'm in class 3A, and I like Mr. Kane."

"That's very nice, Katie," Mr. Rosen said. "But, as grown-ups, we have to make sure school is a place where you can learn."

"But we learned a lot that day," Katie said.

"What could you possibly have learned on a no-rules day?" Mr. Rosen asked.

"We learned that rules are really important." Katie stopped and thought about Mr. Ditherspoon's pencil point rule. "Well, at least *most* rules," she added.

"Really?" Mr. Rosen said with surprise.

Katie nodded. "We even came up with some rules of our own." She turned toward Jeremy and Suzanne. They stood up, too.

"I think it's important to do your homework," Katie began. "And there shouldn't be any fighting in school, either."

"Kids should be able to wear what they want," Suzanne continued. "But no one should be allowed to make fun of someone else's outfit."

"Or their drawings," Katie added. "You shouldn't make fun of anyone for any reason."

"There have to be rules in sports," Jeremy said. "And I think new kids should be paired up with a buddy on their first day of school. Then they could have a friend right away."

"We should have a student government at school," Katie told the school board. "I think kids would follow rules more easily if they got to make some of them."

Katie looked over at Mr. Kane. He didn't

seem so nervous anymore. He seemed proud. The principal stood up and began to clap. Soon most of the parents in the room were on their feet and clapping, too.

Mr. Rosen smiled at the kids. "Well, I guess you did learn something that day," he began.

"Mr. Kane is very smart," Katie told him.

"Yes, he is." Mr. Rosen agreed. He turned toward Mr. Kane. "There's no way we could possibly fire you now."

"Thank you," Mr. Kane said.

"But I do have one question," Mr. Rosen continued. "Why didn't you tell anyone about your plan?"

Mr. Kane gulped. He fiddled with his tie. He looked at his shoes. What could he say? He had no idea what had happened that day.

"Mr. Kane couldn't have told anyone," Katie quickly said. "It *had* to be a surprise. Otherwise, we never would have learned the lesson ourselves."

Everyone started clapping again.

"Good one, Katie," Suzanne whispered. "Grown-ups love when you say stuff like that."

Chapter 12

The meeting didn't last much longer. When it was over, Mr. Kane walked over to Katie, Suzanne, and Jeremy.

"I don't know how to thank you kids," he said. "I'm not quite sure what happened this week. But I am glad it turned out this way. You had some great ideas."

Katie smiled. She thought so, too.

"So who wants ice cream?" Mr. Kane asked. "My treat!"

Talk about a great idea!

As Katie walked outside with her friends and her parents, she felt a breeze hit the back of her neck. Her smile turned to a frown. This was awful. She didn't want to turn into any-one else. She just wanted to stay Katie Carew—and have a big rocky road ice cream cone.

"Whoa, it's getting cold!" Suzanne zipped the front of her sparkly black jacket. "Feel that wind."

Katie smiled brightly. It wasn't the magic wind after all. It was just a plain, old wind. One that could blow on anyone.

"I think it feels wonderful!" she said.

Chapter 13

Class 3A's Favorite Playground Games!

George is the king of Four Square. Suzanne loves to play Statue Tag. Jeremy's favorite game is soccer, but he's always ready to play Poison. Now you and your friends can play these games too. Here's how.

Four Square (a game for four players)

You will need: Chalk, a kickball

You can draw a four square court on any playground. Draw a large square, sixteen feet wide by sixteen feet long. Now divide it into four smaller squares of equal size. The smaller squares should be four feet wide by four feet long. (You can get a grown-up to help you with this part.)

One player stands in each square. One square is called the king. The other squares are called the queen, the prince, and the princess. The king is the highest-ranking square. The princess is the lowest-ranking square.

To start the game, the king serves the ball by bouncing it in his square and then hitting it to any of the other players. That player has to let the ball bounce, and then hit it to any other player. Then that player has to hit the ball to another player.

Keep going until one of these things happens:

*A player hits the ball before it bounces in her square.

*A player does not hit the ball.

*A player hits the ball out of bounds. (The ball has to land in someone's square.)

If anything like that happens, the player

who made the mistake has to move to the princess square. The other players move up to fill the empty squares.

At the end of recess, the player in the king's box is the winner.

Statue Tag (a game for ten or more players)

You will need: chalk

Use the chalk to make a starting line. Then choose one player to be *it*. *It* must stand about fifty feet away from the line with her back to the other players.

It counts to ten. While she's counting, the other players run or walk toward her. As soon as it reaches ten, she turns around.

That's when all the other players stand still like statues. Anyone caught moving (even a little, teensy bit) has to go back to the starting line.

Then *it* turns around and begins to count to ten again.

As soon as any player is close enough to tag *it*, he should. Just be sure her back is turned, because if she sees you moving, you have to go back to the starting line.

The first player to tag *it*, becomes the new *it*.

Poison (a game for five or more players)

You will need: a pot

The players all join hands, making a circle around the pot. One player is chosen to be the leader. He tries to push or pull the other players so that one of them knocks a foot against the pot.

As soon as any player touches the pot, he becomes poison. All the other players have to run away from him. The player who is poison has to try and catch one of the other players. That person becomes the new leader, and the game begins again.

Get Lost!

For my swimming buddies,
Marie and Cathy—N.K.

If you purchased this book without a cover, you should be aware that this book is
stolen property. It was reported as "unsold and destroyed" to the publisher, and neither
the author nor the publisher has received any payment for this "stripped book."

The scanning, uploading, and distribution of this book via the Internet or via any
other means without the permission of the publisher is illegal and punishable by law.
Please purchase only authorized electronic editions and do not participate in
or encourage electronic piracy of copyrighted materials. Your support of the author's
rights is appreciated.

Text copyright © 2003 by Nancy Krulik. Illustrations copyright © 2003 by John and
Wendy. All rights reserved. Published by Grosset & Dunlap, a division of Penguin
Young Readers Group, 345 Hudson Street, New York, NY, 10014. GROSSET & DUNLAP
is a trademark of Penguin Random House LLC.
Manufactured in China

Library of Congress Cataloging-in-Publication Data

Krulik, Nancy E.
Get Lost! / by Nancy Krulik ; illustrated by John & Wendy.
p. cm. — (Katie Kazoo, switcheroo ; 6)
Summary: Katie Carew's third-grade class spends three days at Science Camp, where
Katie magically changes places with the strict Head Counselor while on a hike and gets
her group hopelessly lost. Includes directions for making all natural soap.
[1. Camps—Fiction. 2. Camp counselors—Fiction. 3. Magic—Fiction. 4. Lost
children—Fiction.] I. John, ill. II. Wendy, ill. III. Title. IV. Series: Krulik, Nancy E.
Katie Kazoo, switcheroo ; 6.
PZ7.K944Gc 2003
[Fic]—dc21

2002015624

10 9 8 7 6 5 4 3 2 1

Proprietary ISBN 978-1-101-95131-6
Part of Boxed Set, ISBN 978-1-101-95128-6

Get Lost!

by Nancy Krulik • illustrated by John & Wendy

Grosset & Dunlap

Chapter 1

Katie Carew bent down and kissed her cocker spaniel on the nose. "Don't be afraid, Pepper," she told him. "I'm not going away forever. It's just three days."

Pepper sniffed at Katie's mouth. Then he licked her—right on the lips.

Katie let out a big yawn. It was 7:30 Monday morning. Usually, that was the time Katie got out of bed. But not today. Today Katie had already eaten breakfast. She was already dressed. And she was already at school!

Katie yawned again. She was so tired. She hadn't slept at all the night before. She'd been

1

too nervous. She was about to go away to Science Camp—*for three days and two nights!*

Just then, a big yellow school bus pulled into the parking lot.

"Yahoo! The bus is here!" Manny Gonzalez shouted excitedly. "Science Camp, here we come!"

Katie's class had been talking about Science Camp since the first day of school. The third grade made the trip every year.

Some kids were really excited to go. Katie was more nervous. She had never been away from her family for that long before.

"Hey Katie, are you psyched or what?" Katie's best friend Jeremy Fox called out, as he and his mother walked onto the school playground.

"Or what," Katie answered nervously.

"Come on. Camp is great! I spent two weeks at sleepaway camp last summer. It was the best time of my whole life."

Jeremy was wearing hiking boots and

carrying a water canteen. He'd packed his clothes in a waterproof camp duffel bag. His sleeping bag was made of camouflage material.

Katie was wearing her everyday sneakers. Her mother had packed her clothes in the beat-up suitcase she used when she visited her grandma. Suddenly, Katie's Cuddle Bears sleeping bag seemed kind of babyish.

Katie's mom gave her a big squeeze. "You're going to have a great time. It's only two nights. Think of it as a long sleepover." Mrs. Carew pointed toward the edge of the playground. "Oh, look—here comes Suzanne!"

Suzanne Lock was Katie's other best friend. Katie figured she must have been planning for a *really* long sleepover. After all, she was wheeling a *huge* hot pink suitcase and carrying a small overnight bag. Her father was carrying the matching duffel bag.

Quickly, Katie hurried over to help Suzanne with her bags.

"Why do you have so much stuff?" Katie
asked as she took the overnight bag from her
friend. It was very heavy.

"A girl's got to be prepared for anything,
Katie." Suzanne smiled as she unloaded the
rest of her luggage beside Katie's. "If it's cold

at night, I'll need a jacket. If it's warm during the day, I'll need shorts. And I don't want to wear the same outfit at night that I wore all day, so . . . "

"We're going *camping!*" Jeremy shouted. "You're supposed to rough it!"

"I am! I didn't bring my blow-dryer."

Katie giggled. She was scared to go to Science Camp, but she was glad her two best friends would be there with her. She loved them both—even if they didn't always like each other.

"Hey, Katie, have you seen George?" Kevin Camilleri asked as he came running over. "Manny and I have to talk to him."

"I don't think he's here yet," Katie told him. "What's so important?"

"It's a secret," Kevin said. "We aren't telling anyone but George."

Just then, Mrs. Derkman stepped onto the playground. Katie could hardly believe that this was her teacher. Usually, Mrs. Derkman

wore dresses and high heels. Her hair was always perfect, and she smelled like sweet perfume.

But today, Mrs. Derkman was a mess! She was wearing sweatpants and sneakers. Her hair was covered by a huge, floppy hat. Worst of all, she smelled like bug spray.

"Whoa! Check out Mrs. Derkman!" Kevin shouted. "She looks like a regular person."

A tall man with a beard and moustache walked over to Mrs. Derkman. "Here are your bags, honey," he said. "Your suitcase is so heavy. What do you have in there?"

"Bug spray, bug candles, and bug cream," Mrs. Derkman answered. "Those creatures aren't getting anywhere near me this year!"

"Did you hear him?" Kevin whispered to Katie. "He called Mrs. Derkman *honey*."

"That must be Mr. Derkman," Katie's mom said to Mrs. Fox. "He seems very nice."

Katie gasped. *Mrs. Derkman's husband?*

"We'd better go now," Mrs. Derkman said,

nervously looking at her watch.

Mr. Derkman smiled. "See you in three days," he said. "Don't let the bedbugs bite!"

Mrs. Derkman's eyes bulged. "Don't say that!" she squawked. Then she kissed her husband on the cheek.

The kids stared at their teacher in amaze-ment.

"Okay, class, let's get on the bus!" Mrs. Derkman ordered her class. "We have no time to waste."

Katie sighed. Mrs. Derkman still *sounded* like herself.

"Well, this is it, sweetie," said Katie's mom. "Better get on line."

"You'll stay until the bus leaves?" Katie asked nervously.

Her mom nodded. "Of course, honey."

Katie gave Pepper one last pat, and then headed toward the bus. But before she could get on board, Manny started to yell.

"Mrs. Derkman, we can't leave!" He shouted out. "George isn't here yet!"

The kids all looked around. Where could George Brennan be?

Chapter 2

"Please, Mrs. Derkman, we have to wait!" Manny begged as the class began to board the bus. "Camp won't be fun without George!"

"We still have a few minutes before all the luggage is loaded onto the bus," Mrs. Derkman assured him. "I'm sure George will be here by then."

Katie found a seat near the window in the middle of the bus. Suzanne hopped into the seat beside her.

"Do you think George is coming?" Katie asked Suzanne as the girls buckled their seat belts.

"I won't miss him if he doesn't. George is

always telling dumb jokes," Suzanne said.

Katie frowned. Sometimes Suzanne could be pretty mean. Katie liked George's jokes. They were really funny. She liked George, too. He was the one who had given Katie her extremely cool nickname—Katie Kazoo.

"I hope we don't have to wait around all day for him," Jeremy said, as he took the seat across the aisle from Katie and Suzanne. "I want to get to camp!"

"There he is!" Kevin's voice rang out from the back of the bus. "Hurry up, George!" he shouted through the open window.

But George wasn't hurrying. In fact, it looked as though his dad was dragging him across the playground to the bus. George had a very angry scowl on his face.

Mr. Brennan marched George straight up to the yellow bus. "Have a good time, son," Mr. Brennan said.

"Fat chance," George barked back.

Mr. Brennan sighed. "It's just a few days at

Science Camp, George. It's not like you're joining the army."

George didn't answer. He walked to the back of the bus and plopped down in the seat across from Manny and Kevin.

Kevin smiled at his pal. "Am I glad to see you. You wouldn't believe the amazing things I snuck into my suitcase." Kevin leaned over to whisper in George's ear. "I packed all kinds of practical joke stuff—plastic bugs, pepper gum, and a whoopee cushion."

Usually, George was really into things like whoopee cushions. But not today. He just sat there, staring out the window with his hands crossed over his chest. "Big deal," he muttered.

Kevin looked surprised. "Come on. We're going to have so much fun!"

George shook his head. "No we're not. This whole Science Camp thing is dumb."

Jeremy looked back at him. "You're nuts, George. Camp's the best. "I should know.

I went to camp last summer."

Suzanne sighed. "You've only told us that about a million times."

"Well, I don't think camp's cool," George argued. "Who wants to go to camp when you can sleep in your own bed and have cable TV?"

As the bus drove away, Katie looked out the window and watched her mother become smaller and smaller. Soon, Katie couldn't see her mom at all. A really lonely feeling came over her.

Katie wasn't the only one feeling sad. Katie could see a tear falling down the side of Suzanne's face.

"Hey, you want to share a bunk bed?" Katie asked, trying to cheer her pal.

Suzanne smiled . . . a little. "Can I have the top?"

"Sure."

Jeremy turned to Katie and Suzanne. "You guys want to hear a camp cheer?" he asked.

"Why not?" Suzanne said.

Jeremy smiled broadly as he began to cheer. "Brrr. It's cold in here. There must be 3A in the atmosphere. All hands clap. All feet stamp. We're the coolest kids at Science Camp!"

Soon the kids in class 3A were shouting Jeremy's cheer. Mandy Banks and Miriam Chan were even doing a hand-clapping game to the rhythm. Everyone was having fun.

Everyone except George. He looked miserable.

Katie joined in. She felt a little bit better. As Katie looked over at Jeremy's smiling face, she hoped that she would be as happy at camp as he'd been.

But Katie couldn't help feeling that something awful was going to happen at Science Camp.

Chapter 3

As the bus turned a corner, the kids caught a glimpse of the camp sign. Suddenly, everyone seemed to be talking at once.

Everyone but George, that is. He sat there like a lump.

"We're here, because we're here, because we're here, because we're here . . . " Jeremy began singing another one of his camp songs.

"Ooh, are those the cabins?" Mandy asked, pointing to the tiny little wooden huts that dotted the campgrounds.

"Did you see that lake?" Zoe added. "It's so blue."

"I wonder where the nature shack is,"

Manny said. "Mrs. Derkman told me they have goats and sheep there."

"Do you think they have full-length mirrors in the cabins?" Suzanne asked.

Before Katie could answer, the bus rolled to a stop. Immediately, the kids unbuckled their belts and bolted for the door.

One by one the children filed off the bus. Katie looked around. Science Camp was really pretty. The trees were blossoming. She could hear birds singing in the distance. And there was a clean smell to the breeze that circled gently around her head.

The breeze!

Suddenly Katie had a nervous feeling in the pit of her stomach.

Quickly she looked at her classmates. Their hair was blowing in the wind, too.

She stared at the trees. The leaves and blossoms were moving. *Phew*. It was just a normal, everyday breeze. For a moment there, Katie had been afraid that the *magic wind*

had followed her all the way to Science Camp.

The magic wind was a tornado-like wind that twisted and turned—but only around Katie. It was really scary. But the scariest part happened after the wind *stopped* blowing. That's when Katie turned into someone else!

It all started one really awful day. Katie had ruined her favorite jeans and burped in front of the whole class. That had been so embarrassing. Katie had wished that she could be anyone but herself.

There must have been a shooting star flying overhead or something when she made that wish, because the very next day, the magic wind blew, turning Katie into Speedy, the class hamster! Katie had spent a whole morning gnawing on wooden chew sticks and running on a hamster wheel.

Luckily, Katie had changed back into herself before anyone stepped on her!

Katie never knew who the magic wind might turn her into next. Already it had

switcherooed her into the school lunch lady, Lucille, and the principal, Mr. Kane. And once the magic wind turned Katie into *Jeremy*. What a mess that had been!

Katie never knew when the magic wind was coming. She just hoped that the wind wouldn't be able to find her at Science Camp. It was going to be hard enough being away from home. She didn't want to have to be away from her body, too.

Chapter 4

Manny, George, and Kevin were all huddled together on the grass behind the bus. Manny and Kevin were whispering to each other and giggling. George just looked bored.

Finally, Manny walked up to Mrs. Derkman and stared at her arm. At first, he didn't say anything. Then he asked her, "Mrs. Derkman, what's black and green, has six legs, a furry body, and two antennae?"

Mrs. Derkman shrugged. "I don't know, Manny."

"I don't know either, but it's crawling up your arm!" Manny told her.

"*Aaaahhhhhh!*" Mrs. Derkman screamed

so loud, Katie was sure they could hear her back at Cherrydale Elementary School. The teacher jumped up and down, slapping her arm. "Get it off me! Get it off me right now!"

Suddenly, a woman with a deep, booming voice came up behind Mrs. Derkman. "What is going on here?" she demanded.

Katie gasped. The woman was very tall. Her muscles were bulging out of her green army uniform. She looked like she never smiled . . . ever. She seemed scarier than any bug.

"Th-th-there's a hairy bug on my arm," Mrs. Derkman stammered.

"Oh, give me a break," the woman in the army uniform barked. "Bugs are part of life out here. Get used to it, soldier."

Soldier?

Mrs. Derkman looked at her curiously. "Excuse me?" she asked.

"Um . . . I mean, there's nothing on your arm," the woman said.

Mrs. Derkman glanced at her bugless arm and sighed. "George Brennan, come here!"

George moped his way over toward the teacher. "I didn't do anything," he insisted.

"Maybe not. But I have a feeling that was your idea of a joke," Mrs. Derkman said.

"It wasn't. Honest," George insisted.

"I wouldn't worry about any more jokes." The woman in the uniform assured Mrs. Derkman. "I'm Genie Manzini, the head counselor. I don't allow for any joking at Science Camp." Genie glared at George.

"Maybe we should call her Genie the *Meanie,*" Suzanne whispered to Katie.

Katie wanted to laugh, but she didn't dare. Who knew what Genie the Meanie might do?

"Okay troops . . . I mean, *boys and girls,*" Genie corrected herself. "I want you to meet the staff. To begin with, I am the head counselor. *Everyone* here answers to me."

The children all turned around to see what Mrs. Derkman would say to that. Mrs. Derkman didn't like answering to anyone.

But Mrs. Derkman didn't seem to have heard anything Genie had said. She was too busy spraying herself with bug spray. "Get off

me, you miserable ant!" The teacher muttered as she sprayed her sneaker.

Genie pointed to a small woman with short brown hair and a cheery smile. "This is Tess," she said. "She runs our animal program."

"Hi everyone," Tess greeted them. "I hope you will all visit the nature shack and help with the animals."

Katie grinned. Tess seemed nice. And maybe visiting the animals in the nature shack would keep her from missing Pepper so much.

"And this is Carson, our nature arts instructor," Genie said, pointing to a tall, thin man wearing sunglasses and a tie-dyed T-shirt.

"You won't believe all the things we can create with nature's art supplies," Carson told them. "We're going to have fun here, right?"

"Right!" the kids shouted back.

Genie did not look pleased.

Just then, a loud bell rang out over the campground. "Okay, that means chow time,"

Genie told them. "You have exactly twenty-seven minutes for lunch. Now line up."

The kids formed a straight line.

"March," Genie ordered. "Hup, two, three, four. Hup, two, three . . . "

As Katie marched toward the mess hall, she remembered what George's father had said about Science Camp not being the army.

Mr. Brennan couldn't have been more wrong.

Chapter 5

Genie the Meanie kept the kids moving all day long. They went from morning to night without a rest. Some of the activities—like making beeswax candles and feeding the animals—were kind of fun.

But Genie never once let the kids forget that Science Camp was part of school. She made them carry notebooks and pencils everywhere, so they could take notes on what they learned.

"I'm exhausted," Katie said as she flopped down on the bottom bunk.

"All I know is Science Camp made me really tired," Miriam added. "I think I could fall

asleep anywhere. Even on this lumpy bed."

Suzanne put her foot on the metal edge of Katie's bed and hopped up onto her top bunk.

The top bunk sagged slightly over Katie's head. The sagging lump moved back and forth as Suzanne found a comfortable spot to lie down. For a minute, Katie thought the bed might come down on top of her.

It was easier not to look up, so instead Katie looked around the cabin. There were four bunk beds lined up along the walls. The walls of the cabin were made of pine-colored wood paneling. There were four screened-in windows on each wall.

Just then, the cabin door swung open. "Okay, girls, it's time for lights out," Tess said, as she walked in and flicked off the light.

As Tess left the cabin, Katie felt scared . . . and lonely. Pepper always slept on her bed with her at home. Now she was all alone.

Suddenly, Katie heard leaves rustling outside the bunk. "Suzanne," she whispered.

"Do you hear that?"

Suzanne listened for a second. "I think there's someone out there."

"Someone or some*thing*," Miriam suggested nervously.

Zoe leaped out of her bed and ran over to

where Katie was sleeping. "Do you mind if I just sit here?" she asked Katie. "I don't think I want to be so close to the door."

The crunching of the leaves was louder now. Whatever was out there was getting closer.

"Do you think it's a bear?" Katie asked.

"Maybe it's a monster," Mandy suggested. "A monster who hates kids at Science Camp."

Suddenly, a huge light beam came shining in through the cabin window.

"*Aaaaaaaaaahhhhhhhhh!*" The girls all screamed. "It's the Science Camp monster!"

But the light wasn't coming from a monster. It was coming from Genie the Meanie's flashlight.

"All right, boys, I see you out there," Genie shouted. "You've been bunkhopping!"

The girls all raced to the windows to see what was happening. In the glare of Genie's light, they could see Kevin and Manny's faces.

"I've got the perfect punishment for you two," Genie assured them in a voice that made the boys shake.

The head counselor grabbed Manny by the hand and walked him over to a huge old pine tree. "Hug it!" Genie ordered.

"Hug what?" Manny asked.

"The tree. *Hug the tree,*" Genie ordered again. She turned to Kevin. "You hug the one next to it. That way I can be sure you boys aren't going anywhere."

Kevin had no choice. He reached out his arms and hugged the tree. Manny did the same.

The girls knew they were supposed to be quiet after lights out. But they couldn't help it. The sight of Manny and Kevin hugging trees was just too funny. They all started to laugh.

And Genie the Meanie didn't tell them to stop.

Chapter 6

"What's that sticky stuff in your hair?"
Carson asked Kevin, as everyone entered the
mess hall for breakfast the next morning.

"Pine sap," Kevin replied.

"How'd you get that on your head?" the
nature arts counselor asked.

Kevin moaned and tried to wipe his hair. "I
don't want to talk about it."

Kevin took his tray and sat down beside
Katie, Jeremy, Suzanne, and Manny.

"What's up with George?" Suzanne asked
Kevin. "I thought you guys always sat
together."

It was true. George, Manny, and Kevin

usually did everything together.

But today, George was sitting all by him-self in the back of the mess hall. He looked miserable.

"I don't know what his problem is," Manny said. "He doesn't want to do anything. Like last night. We were all telling ghost stories in the cabin. George went to sleep!'"

"That doesn't sound like George," Katie agreed. "He loves scary stuff."

"So, Jeremy, when exactly is this place going to get fun?" Suzanne asked, changing the subject. "You keep talking about how great camp is, but I think Science Camp is a real drag."

Jeremy nodded. "This isn't like the camp I went to last summer," he agreed. "But maybe today we'll get to to play some games or some-thing."

Just then, Genie passed by the table. Jeremy smiled nervously in her direction. "Excuse me, Genie."

The head counselor glared down at him. "What is it soldier . . . I mean *student?*"

"Are we going to have some free time today?" Jeremy asked. "Maybe we can play soccer or basketball or something. You know, have a little fun."

Genie's eyes opened wide. "This is not summer camp!" she shouted. "This is Science Camp. You are not here to play. You are here to learn. And nobody said learning has to be fun!"

Jeremy gulped. Genie sure sounded mad.

"I have a full schedule for you kids," she continued. "It begins with inspection. I'm going to check each of your cabins for neatness. And your beds had better be made well. I want those sheets pulled so tight I can bounce a quarter off them!"

"What does bouncing quarters on beds have to do with science?" Manny wondered aloud, after Genie walked away.

As the kids chowed down on their eggs,

Katie glanced over at George. He seemed very quiet. She was worried about him. Finally, she got up and walked over to sit beside her friend.

"Hey, George," Katie greeted him.

George didn't say anything. He just shoved a forkful of eggs into his mouth. "These are gross," he muttered between bites.

"I know egg-zactly what you mean," Katie joked.

George didn't laugh. Instead, he took another forkful of eggs.

"Are you looking forward to our hike this afternoon?" Katie asked, changing the subject.

George rolled his eyes. "No," he snapped. "Hikes are dumb. Everything here is dumb."

"George, why are you being so mean?"

"I'm not being mean. I'm just too cool for this place," George told her. "Can I help it if you're not?"

Katie's face got red. "That was a mean

thing to say, George Brennan!" she shouted. "I don't think you're cool at all. I think you're a jerk!"

Then, Katie got up and stormed out of the mess hall—before Mrs. Derkman had a chance to tell her that *jerk* isn't a word you use in school.

Chapter 7

After Genie had inspected their cabins, the kids in 3A gathered on the main lawn to get ready for their hikes. They each had their own water bottles and a bag of cookout food to carry.

Cookie, the camp cook, smiled at Katie as she handed her a bag. "There's no meat in yours," she assured Katie. Cookie knew that Katie was a vegetarian. "But I added extra carrot sticks and potato chips. I don't let kids go hungry."

"Thanks," Katie said with a grin.

The class had been split into small groups for their hikes. Katie, Suzanne, Jeremy and

George were in the same group.

"Who's our leader, anyway?" George asked. "Mrs. Derkman," Suzanne said.

Katie frowned. " I was hoping Tess or Carson could be our leader."

Just then Genie walked toward Katie and her friends. "Mrs. Derkman has a bad case of poison ivy," she told them. "She fell in a patch of it while running away from an oncoming fly. I'll be taking you on your hike.

"Okay, troops. March," Genie ordered. "Left, right, left, right."

Katie got in line behind George. He was going very slowly. "You'd better march faster," Katie told him. "Genie the Meanie is going to yell at you."

George reached into his pocket and pulled out a hard candy wrapped in shiny paper. "What's the hurry?" he mumbled as he sucked on the candy. "It's not like we're going any-where. It's a hike to nowhere."

"We're supposed to be looking at the

plants and animals in the woods," Katie reminded him. "See, there's a chipmunk." George was not impressed.

After they'd been hiking for a while, Katie marched up to the front of the line. "Genie," she asked quietly. "Are we anywhere near a bathroom?"

Genie pointed out into the woods.

"Behind that tree. Or that tree. Or any tree," Genie told her.

Katie gulped. "You mean I have to pee in the woods?"

Genie nodded. "Or hold it in."

That settled it. Katie ran off in the direction of a huge oak tree surrounded by some high shrubs. She hoped the bushes would hide her.

Suddenly, Katie felt a cold breeze on the back of her neck. The light wind felt great after the long hike she'd been on . . .until Katie realized that the wind wasn't blowing anywhere but on her.

This was no ordinary wind. This was the magic wind!

Oh no, Katie thought. *Not here. Not in the middle of the woods!*

The magic wind began spinning faster and faster, all around Katie. She shut her eyes tightly, and tried not to cry. As the fierce tornado swirled, she held on to the tree. She

struggled to keep her feet on the ground. The wind just kept getting more and more powerful.

And then it stopped.

Katie was afraid to open her eyes. What if the wind had blown her away. What if she was all alone in the middle of the forest?

But Katie was *not* alone. The other kids were right nearby.

As Katie opened her eyes, Jeremy stared up at her.

"Genie?" he asked. "Why are you hugging that tree?"

Chapter 8

Katie looked down at her feet. Instead of her own bright red sneakers, she saw Genie's hiking boots. And she was wearing army pants instead of jeans.

Katie had become Genie the Meanie!

Uh-oh. Genie was in charge of the hike. She was supposed to teach the kids to build a fire, cook the food, and find the way back to camp.

Katie didn't know how to do any of those things.

"Hey, what happened to Katie?" George asked. "She's been gone a long time."

Katie gulped. She knew exactly where Katie was. But how could she explain that to her friends?

"Katie!" Jeremy called into the woods.

There was no answer.

"Katie Kazoo, quit goofing around," George shouted.

Suzanne began to panic. "She's missing!"

"Relax, she didn't go far," Katie assured her. "I'm sure if we just sit here she'll come back."

Suzanne was so scared she forgot to be afraid of Genie the Meanie. "We can't just sit here!" she declared. "She's lost in the woods somewhere. We've got to look for her!"

Katie didn't know what to do. The real Genie probably would have searched for her. That was her job—to keep everyone safe.

"All right. We'll look for your friend. But let's be sure to stick together. I don't want to lose any more of you," Katie said, trying to sound like the real Genie the Meanie.

As the kids wandered through the woods, searching for their missing friend, Katie tried her best to act like a real head counselor. It wasn't easy. Katie had never been out in the woods before.

The kids were starting to panic. Katie had to do something to calm them down. She decided to change the subject. That's what a real head counselor would do—get the kids thinking about something else.

Katie pointed to a patch of leaves on the ground. Each of the green leaves had three parts. "Look at that beautiful plant," Katie said. She bent down to pick up a leaf.

"Genie, don't touch that!" Jeremy shouted. "That's poison ivy."

Oops! Katie gulped. What a mistake that would have been.

"Very good, Jeremy," Katie said. "I *meant* to do that. It was a test. I wanted to see if you kids could recognize poison ivy."

"I don't want to look at leaves," Suzanne

moaned. "I want to look for Katie."

"Or what's left of Katie," George added.

"Cut that out, George!" Suzanne shouted.

"Make me!" George screamed back.

Katie leaped between them. "Let's just keep walking," she ordered.

"Which way?" George groaned.

Katie led the kids down a dirt path. "Maybe she headed east," Katie told the kids. "We'll try that way."

"Uh, Genie," Jeremy interrupted, as Katie turned to her right. "We're actually heading west."

"How do you know?" Katie asked him.

"It's almost sunset. The sun sets in the west. It's in front of us right now."

Katie sighed. She didn't know any of this stuff. "Of course," Katie said. "I meant west. We'll head west."

"It's getting kind of dark," Suzanne moaned, as the kids walked behind Katie.

"That's just a cloud over the sun," Katie

assured her, trying to sound confident.

"Actually, I think it's getting dark because it's about six o'clock," Jeremy told her. "It'll be night soon."

"Oh, no!" Suzanne shouted. "Katie will be all alone in the woods at night!"

"Relax, Suzanne," Katie said. "We'll find your friend."

"Katie's not just any friend," Suzanne said. "She's my best friend. I'm worried about her." She looked at George and Jeremy. "Which is more than I can say for some people."

"Hey, she's my best friend, too," Jeremy argued.

"But you don't sound very worried," Suzanne told him.

"I am too worried," Jeremy said.

Katie sighed. "Please stop . . .Whoa!" Before Katie could finish her sentence, she went sliding down a long, slippery slope. When she reached the bottom, she found herself waist deep in thick, gooey mud!

"*Help!* Quicksand!" Katie shouted out. She looked up at George, Jeremy, and Suzanne. "I'm sinking! Help me!"

George stared down at the head counselor. "I'm not helping her," he told Jeremy and Suzanne. "Let the quicksand swallow her up."

"But she's the only one who knows the way back to camp!" Suzanne declared. "And now she's sinking into quicksand!"

"She's not sinking," Jeremy assured her. "And that's not quicksand. It's just a mud-slide. We played on one of those at my summer camp. Genie, just grab on to that tree branch and pull yourself back up the hill." Katie did as she was told. She grabbed on to a low-lying branch and tried to pull herself up. It wasn't easy. The mud had made her hands slippery, and the hill was steep.

"Whoa!" Katie cried out, as she slipped back down the mudslide. She fell backward, tripped over a rock, and went rolling into the woods.

Finally, she landed in a thick pile of leaves. Frantically, Katie tried to find a path back up the hill. But there was mud every-where. Every time she tried to move up the hill, she'd slide back down.

And then, suddenly, she felt a familiar breeze hit the back of her neck.

The magic wind was back!

Wild tornado-like gusts swirled all around Katie's body. She grasped at a nearby tree, but it was out of her reach.

Bam! The strong wind knocked Katie off her feet. She fell to the ground with a *thud*. The wind was the fiercest it had ever been. Katie grabbed on to a huge rock. Her feet flew up in the air, but she refused to let go of that rock. She held on tightly.

And then the wind stopped.

Everything around her was perfectly calm.

Everything except Genie the Meanie, that is. She was lying on the ground, clutching a rock. And she wasn't at all

sure how she'd gotten there.

Genie looked down at her clothes. Her army pants were covered with mud. "What happened? What's going on here?" Genie barked to Katie, who was now standing beside her.

Katie knew she had to say something. "I'm so glad you found me," she blurted out. "I've been lost so long. You're a great counselor, Genie."

"*Head* counselor," Genie reminded her. She scrambled to her feet. Then she looked at Katie curiously. "You were lost?" she asked.

Katie grinned. "Of course. How else could you have found me?"

Chapter 9

"Okay, soldier, just another few feet," Genie shouted back to Katie. "Try to climb at the same time I do." Genie had wrapped her belt around Katie's waist. She was using the belt to tow Katie up the slippery hill.

Katie planted her feet firmly into the mud and tried to climb. "This is hard," she moaned.

"Almost there," Genie assured her.

"Hey, look," George cried out. "It's Katie Kazoo!"

As Katie and Genie wandered back toward the others, Jeremy raced over to them. "Where were you?" he demanded.

"I went into the woods to . . .to . . ."

"She went to pee." George giggled.

Katie blushed. "Anyway, I got lost, and Genie found me."

"Just in time," George said. "I'm starving. We never got to have our cookout because we were looking for you. Let's just get back to camp and eat something."

"Which way do we go?" Jeremy asked.

Genie's eyes confidently scanned the trees. Suddenly, her face fell. "Where are the red ribbons?" she muttered.

"What ribbons?" Katie asked.

"The red ribbons!" Genie exclaimed, sounding very nervous. "The ones that are tied to the trees. They mark the path back to camp."

"We must have wandered off the path when we were looking for Katie," Jeremy thought aloud. "Can't we take another path?"

"We could," Genie agreed, "if I knew one. But I have no idea how far we are from camp

or which way to turn to go back. I'm not even sure how we got here. It's all sort of a blur."

"This is all your fault, Katie Kazoo," George snapped.

Katie stared at George. Did he know that it was she, not Genie, who had gotten them lost? Did George know about magic wind?

"If you hadn't disappeared, we wouldn't have had to look for you," George continued.

Okay, so George didn't know about the magic wind. But he was right. She was the reason the kids were lost. And now even Genie couldn't get them back safely.

"I hate the dark. I hate it," Suzanne blubbered. "We don't even have a flashlight."

"What if there really is a Science Camp monster out there? He could get us." George's eyes grew big. His lip quivered, but he didn't cry. He just stared out into the woods.

Even Jeremy seemed nervous. "Do you think the other kids in our class are worried about us?" he asked.

"Maybe they'll call the police to come look for us," Suzanne said.

"I'll bet Mrs. Derkman is a total wreck," George added. "You know how she can get."

"I doubt it," Katie said. "I'll bet she's fine. She knows we're with the head counselor. Genie can take care of us."

Hoot!

"What was that?" Genie cried out.

Katie gulped. Maybe Genie wouldn't be able to take care of them after all. It seemed that even the head counselor was scared to be in the woods at night.

"I think it was an owl," Katie told her. "Tess said there were a lot of owls in these woods. Don't worry, owls won't hurt you."

Grrrr. Just then, everyone heard a loud grumbling noise.

"Now what was *that?*" Genie wailed.

Katie giggled. "George's stomach."

"It always makes that noise when I'm hungry," George moaned.

"Well, we still have all our cookout supplies," Jeremy suggested. "We could eat. All we have to do is build a fire."

"I don't know how," Suzanne said. "My dad always does the grilling at our house."

The kids looked to Genie for help, but the head counselor was busy staring into the woods. "Where are those ribbons?" she kept saying over and over. "I need my ribbons."

"We're going to have to do this ourselves," Katie told her friends. She was trying to act like a head counselor. After all, she'd been Genie—for a little while, anyway. "Jeremy, did they teach you to make a fire at your camp?"

Jeremy nodded. "I can build one. But we're not allowed to use matches, remember?"

"Genie can handle that," Katie said. "You just tell us how to do the rest."

Jeremy pointed to some fallen branches nearby. "Suzanne, you and Katie go collect sticks. Start with little twigs, and then get bigger ones. Make sure the wood is dry.

George, you and I will get some wood, too."

Before long, the kids had plenty of wood. Jeremy showed them how to build a little box of twigs. Genie lit the twigs with her matches. Then she and Jeremy built up the fire, by throwing logs onto the flames.

There was plenty of food to cook. Jeremy, Suzanne, and George cooked hot dogs on

sticks. Katie ate carrot sticks and potato chips. Then the kids toasted marshmallows.

Genie didn't eat anything. She just sat by the fire, staring into the woods.

When the kids were finished with their food, Katie turned to Genie. "We should put the fire out, right?" she asked.

Genie nodded. She seemed to have finally calmed down. At least she wasn't mumbling about the red ribbons anymore. "We shouldn't leave it burning while we sleep," she told Katie.

"Sleep?" Suzanne asked. "Sleep where?"

Genie emptied her canteen of water on the fire. Katie and Jeremy did the same. "We're going to have to sleep here tonight," Genie told the kids, as the last of the flames disappeared. It was dark now. The moon was the only light they had.

"Sleep on the hard ground?" Suzanne asked. "With all that dirt?"

"What's the matter?" Jeremy asked her.

"You didn't bring the right clothes for sleeping outside?"

Suzanne made a face, but didn't say anything.

Katie grabbed a paper garbage bag and began filling it with soft leaves.

"What are you doing?" Suzanne asked her.

"Making a pillow," she answered.

That seemed like a good idea. The kids all grabbed bags and began to make their own pillows. Katie made an extra one for Genie. She felt bad for her. None of this had really been her fault.

Katie yawned. Her eyes were feeling heavy. She lay down and put her head on her pillow. Before she knew what was happening, Katie was asleep.

Chapter 10

Katie hadn't been asleep very long when she heard footsteps in the woods. There was someone prowling around the campsite!

Katie looked at Genie. She was curled up in a ball, snoring away. She wasn't going to be any help.

Now a quiet sniffling noise was coming from where the fire had been.

Slowly, Katie stood and walked in the direction of the sniffles.

There was George. He was wide awake— and he'd been crying.

"George, what's wrong?" she asked him.

George wiped his nose with his sleeve.

"Nothing," he mumbled.

"Come on, George," Katie urged. "I know something's wrong."

"You're gonna laugh" he said quietly.

"No, I won't. I promise."

"I'm scared," George whispered. "I've never been away from home before."

Katie understood that feeling perfectly. Now she knew why George had acted so

grumpy. He didn't want anyone to know.

"You won't tell, will you?" he begged.

"Never." Katie looked around. Everyone else was sleeping. "I have a great idea. Let's stay up all night and see the sun rise.

George smiled a little. "We can tell jokes and stories and stuff."

"Okay," Katie agreed. "Want to see a neat trick?" She put on the hood of her sweatshirt. Then she pulled the strings really tight so the hood closed around her face.

"That's funny," George said. "You look like a faceless monster."

"A faceless Science Camp monster," Katie giggled.

"Do you know what fairy tale gives a monster the shivers?" George asked her.

Katie shook her head.

"Ghoul-dilocks and the Three Brrrrs!" he laughed at his own joke.

Katie grinned. George was back to normal.

One problem solved.

Chapter 11

The next morning, the group was up early. They wanted to get back to camp right away.

"Can you find the right path now?" Jeremy asked Genie hopefully.

"I'm not sure," she replied.

Katie could tell that her friends were getting scared again. But somehow, things seemed less frightening in the sunlight.

"I'm hungry," George moaned. "Do we have any food left from last night? Maybe a hot dog or something?"

Suzanne made a face. "Hot dogs for breakfast? Yuck!"

"I'll eat anything when I'm this starved," George told her.

Katie checked the food pack. It was empty. "We don't have any food left,"

George looked upset. Then, suddenly, he brightened. "Yes, we do," he said. "I have those candies I brought on the hike."

At first Genie seemed angry. "You brought candy on the hike?" Then her stomach growled. "I'll take one," she added.

George reached into his pocket. Then he frowned as he pulled out an empty hand. "This is terrible!"

"What?" Katie asked. "Did you finish them all?"

George shook his head. "There's a hole in my pocket. The candies fell out."

"Oh, no!" Jeremy moaned. "That's awful."

Just then, Katie spotted a shiny round object over by a tree. A few feet away she saw another one . . . and then another. Katie raced over and picked up one of the shiny things.

"It's not awful at all," she told the others.

"George just saved us!"

"How did I do that?" he asked her.

"These are your candies," Katie told him, holding up a shiny wrapped treat. "They must have been falling out of your pocket the whole time we were hiking. All we have to do is follow the trail of candies. They'll lead us back to camp. And we can eat as we hike," she added, popping a butterscotch into her mouth.

Chapter 12

The tired hikers arrived back at camp before their friends woke up. In fact, the whole camp was still asleep—except for Cookie. She was waiting for them outside the Mess Hall.

"Where have you all been?" she asked, as Genie and the kids walked onto the camp-grounds. "I was up all night worrying. If you didn't come back soon, I was going to have to send out a search party."

"It's a long story," Genie told Cookie.

"We got lost. We slept in the woods. And now we're back," Jeremy explained.

"Well, it's sure good to see you," Cookie told them. "Why don't you all take showers? Then

I'll make you a special treat for breakfast. You look starved."

That sounded great to Katie. She was really hungry.

"There's something else I have to do first," George said, as he ran off in the direction of the cabins.

"You know, that was actually kind of fun," Jeremy told Katie and Suzanne as they walked.

"Wait until the other kids hear what a wimp Genie turned out to be!" Suzanne laughed.

Katie shook her head. "I don't think we should tell the other kids about that. It's not nice to make fun of her for being scared."

"But she acted so tough before . . ." Suzanne began.

"She was just doing her job," Katie told her. "She had to be tough. It's a lot of responsibility being a head counselor. You're in charge of everything."

Before Suzanne could argue, the kids heard a loud scream coming from one of the cabins.

"*Spider. . . on my pillow!*"

Mrs. Derkman came racing out of her cabin. Her face was dotted with big blobs of pink lotion. Her hair was wrapped up in curlers. She was wearing a polka-dot flannel nightgown and a pair of fuzzy yellow slippers. She looked awful.

"Wow, check out Mrs. Derkman!" Suzanne exclaimed.

"Oh, no!" Katie gasped.

Jeremy couldn't say anything. He was laughing too hard.

As Mrs. Derkman stood in the middle of the campground screaming, George snuck out of her cabin with a big smile on his face. He ran off before the teacher could spot him.

Katie glanced at Genie. She was looking right in the direction of Mrs. Derkman's cabin. There was no way she could have

missed seeing George run out of there.

Katie frowned. Was Genie going to punish George?

But Genie didn't yell or even call George over. Instead, she walked over to Katie and her friends, and laughed along with them.

Chapter 13

Katie was really sad when the time came to get on the bus and drive back to Cherrydale. Science Camp had been really fun. She was going to miss the bunnies in the nature shack and Cookie's chocolate-chip cookies.

But mostly Katie was going to miss Genie.

It turned out that the head counselor could be really nice when she wanted to. She taught the kids how to melt chocolate and marshmallows on graham crackers to make s'mores. And she showed them how to make beads out of clay that they dug from the ground.

"Maybe we can come back here again in fourth grade," Katie said to Suzanne, as they took seats in the back of the bus.

"That would be so cool," Suzanne agreed. "We could teach everyone how to build a fire."

Just then, Katie felt someone knocking on the window beside her. It was Genie.

Katie opened the window. "Thanks so much," she said. "I really learned a lot."

Genie grinned. "So did I. I learned that kids can do a whole lot for themselves . . . if you give them the chance."

As the bus drove off, Katie felt a cool breeze blow on her through the open window. She was pretty sure it wasn't a magic wind. But she reached up and shut the window— just in case.

No sense taking any chances.

Chapter 14

Science Camp definitely was a fun time. The nature arts counselor had lots of great ideas for nature projects the kids could do. Everyone in class 3A came home with natural soaps that they made all by themselves.

You can make your own Science Camp soap on a rope. Here's how.

Soap on a Rope

You will need:

3 cups Ivory Snow detergent or other soap flakes

bowl

liquid food coloring

1 cup water

vegetable oil

a thin piece of rope

Here's what you do: Pour the soap flakes
into a bowl. Put a few drops of food coloring
in the water. Pour the water onto the soap
flakes. Use your hands to mix the contents of
the bowl until they feel like clay or dough.
Massage a drop or two of vegetable oil into
the palms of your hands. Now shape the soap
anyway you like. Tie the ends of the rope
together. Gently push the knotted end of the
rope into your finished soap shape. Let the
soap stand overnight to set.